EDEN

JOHNS HOPKINS: POETRY AND FICTION
John T. Irwin, General Editor

Poetry Titles in the Series

John Hollander, *"Blue Wine" and Other Poems*

Robert Pack, *Waking to My Name: New and Selected Poems*

Philip Dacey, *The Boy under the Bed*

Wyatt Prunty, *The Times Between*

Barry Spacks, *Spacks Street: New and Selected Poems*

Gibbons Ruark, *Keeping Company*

David St. John, *Hush*

Wyatt Prunty, *What Women Know, What Men Believe*

Adrien Stoutenberg, *Land of Superior Mirages: New and Selected Poems*

John Hollander, *In Time and Place*

Charles Martin, *Steal the Bacon*

John Bricuth, *The Heisenberg Variations*

Tom Disch, *Yes, Let's: New and Selected Poems*

Wyatt Prunty, *Balance as Belief*

Tom Disch, *Dark Verses and Light*

Ellen Akins, *World like a Knife*

Emily Grosholz, *Eden*

EMILY GROSHOLZ *Eden*

The Johns Hopkins University Press
Baltimore and London

This book has been brought to publication with the generous assistance of the Albert Dowling Trust.

The Johns Hopkins University Press
701 West 40th Street
Baltimore, Maryland 21211-2190
The Johns Hopkins Press Ltd., London

Library of Congress Cataloging-in-Publication Data

Grosholz, Emily, 1950–
　　Eden / Emily Grosholz.
　　　　p.　　cm. — (Johns Hopkins, poetry and fiction)
　　ISBN 0-8018-4389-8 (hc). — ISBN 0-8018-4390-1 (pbk).
　　I. Title.　II. Series.
PS3557.R567E34　1992
811'.54 — dc20　　　　　　　　　　　　　　　　91-44180

The author would like to acknowledge prior publication of the following poems: "On Spadina Avenue," "Dark Tents and Fires," "Rain or Shine," "Autumn Sonata," and "Letter from Toronto" in *The Hudson Review;* "Life of a Salesman" in *New England Review;* "Excursion to the Third *Calanque,*" "Proportions of the Heart," and "The Shape of Desire" in *New Virginia Review;* "Two Passages from Colette" in *Partisan Review;* "Pilgrims" and "The Neolithic Revolution of 1956" in *Pequod;* "Athens Bus Station" and "Waiting for News of Jackie's Firstborn" in *Pivot;* "Thirty-six Weeks" in *Poetry;* "Sidonie" and "63, rue Mirabeau" in *Prairie Schooner;* "Symmetry" and "The Pot of Basil" in *Raritan;* "Listening" and "The Sailboat" in *Sewanee Theological Review;* and "Back Trouble" and "Commuter Marriage" in *The Southern Review.* She is also grateful to the Ingram Merrill Foundation and the Guggenheim Foundation for their support of this book, and to friends in Buffalo who helped shape many of these poems.

To Bob and Benjamin; and to Anne, Dinny, Jim, and Tess,
in loco parentis.

CONTENTS

Flower, Sailboat, Child

Lighted Windows

ON SPADINA AVENUE

Driven by love and curiosity,
I entered the painted shops along Toronto's
Chinatown, and lingered
in one red pharmacy, where every label
was printed in mysterious characters.
Beside myself, not knowing what I stopped for,
I read the scrolling dragons, roots, and flowers
intelligible as nature,
and quizzed the apothecary on her products.

Lovesick for my husband. She was puzzled,
for how could I explain
my private fevers to a perfect stranger?
I questioned her obliquely, hit-or-miss:
Lady, what's this button full of powder?
What's this ointment in the scaly tube?
Who are these dry creatures in the basket
and how are they applied?
The deer tails gleamed in fat, uneven rows,
unrolled sea horses darkened on the shelves,
and other customers with clearer motives
stepped in behind my back.

I couldn't say, his troublesome male beauty
assails me sometimes, watching him at night
next to the closet door
half-dressed, or naked on the bed beside me.
An evening amorousness keeps me awake

for hours brooding, even after love:
how fast in time we are,
how possibly my love could quit this world
and pull down half of heaven when he goes.

The patient Chinese lady has no cure,
and serves her other customers in order.
Across the curled-up, quiet, ochre lizards,
giant starfish, quince, and ginger root,
she turns to look at me.
We both know I'm not ill with this or that,
but suffer from a permanent condition,
a murmur of the heart, the heart itself
calling me out of dreams
to verify my warm, recurrent husband
who turns and takes me in his arms again
and sleepily resumes his half of heaven.

WEST WIND I

I like to wake beside my husband's
large resilient body, surfaces
my hand rehearses out of pure
and pleasurable habit, consciously,
especially where his intersecting planes
make saddle-passes in the uncertain
alps of darkness pitched across our bed:
where his neck and shoulders join,
his back shades into haunches, or his thigh
looms into underbelly with a curve
shaped by the most magnetic zone
my fingers graze, in passing for the moment.

I know each juncture by its hidden odor
caught in the dark brown bear-fur of a blond
that sunlight easily spins to gold:
basil, eucalyptus, harsh vanilla
queen anne's lace, cache of wisteria.
His sweet breath riffles on my cheek
as if day returning were the earth's
lost children coming back again in April.
Who would wake from such a real
and ramifying dream? I switch the tongue
of our alarming clock from lark
to nightingale, and wait with open eyes.

COMMUTER MARRIAGE

I.

Late February snow, and more to come.
No music in my bones, no bounce
in the soft elastic tissue of my heart.
The beat's uneven, pushing yesterday
into tomorrow. Is this all I am?
A membrane flattening and rounding
hooked to a calcium trellis
blood and anima go rustling through.
One breath. Another breath. How many times?

Soul scrapes at contradiction
like a bird against the window. Listen:
thrill of brittle feathers on the glass,
scritch of a leathery claw. Oh let me in,
keeper of summer's house,
in to Tobago or the Carolinas
where sunset burns like driftwood, hot
on the horizontal coals
under the Delft-blue patterned tile of skywall.

I just don't want to hit the road again,
driven by finitude from my dear husband,
skirting the stricken hills
where people seem to homestead in a daze
half-unintentionally.
As if they settled there like snow
beside the crooked road's decline
midway between Altoona and St. Mary's,
Bradford and Kane.

II.

Wrapped in my solitude, I sleep
across hundreds of miles,
and dream of my love on the highway
driving to see me, driving away
again in the chilly darkness.

He listens to news fade in and out
of the small towns he passes,
Salamanca, Dubois, Bradford,
each at the heart of a cloud
of radio waves, invisible.

He hums offkey to the local classical
stations that swell and falter,
or a slow James Taylor ballad
on the popular bands he catches at last
in the ambit of Buffalo.

When he reaches the other side, he calls
and we try to touch by our voices
over the crossing wires, the miles
of folded and swirling air,
of blooming and drystick meadows.

Nothing here repairs his absence,
not his hovering voice, not even
his smile on the bedside photograph,
not sunlight, clouds, or hours.
So I must take my mending down,

and stitch a stray thought to its end.
But underneath my breath I hum
one voice of a two-part round,
and sometimes in my dreams I sing
both melodies out loud.

III.

Elm trees in the early close
of winter take me by surprise
as dusk descends,
take on, without my leave
or wish, the color mauve.

A trick of atmosphere,
earth breathing an upward cloud,
or my imposed desire,
or rising sap that swells
to leaf in winter buds?

Elm tree, shape of my desire,
what is color's origin?
Perhaps the sun's
light reflex as it moves
under the world again.

Midweek I live alone.
Desires rise and fade
with nowhere else to go.
Lengthening day, the empty vases
fill and overflow.

IV.

Like characters in some fantastic opera,
we met in Pittsburgh, Boston, Binghamton,
my love and I, and Sundays sadly parted
at crossroads, bus stops, railway loggias,
in Newark's cloudpots, where the airplanes ply
their version of migration,
scheduled, unseasonal.

Long weekends, short ones, every parting paid
in the currency of patience and regret,
midweek's recitativo building towards
the arias of Saturday and Sunday.
Mostly we drove, as if our cars were mobile
musical anterooms
between divided houses.

Morning light came up, or dusk was falling
as I'd pull in or out of that riverside
unfashionable city with its bridges,
Olmstead parks, and monumental graveyards.
Verdi played in the background, and I wept
to Sills' high reinvention
of Violetta's trials.

Croce e delizia. What mysterious power
love has to drive us wandering over miles
of dingy wilderness in search of home.
Papageno's right: the hell with drama
and squeezing life from monsters. What we want
is wine with a square meal
and close at hand, a spouse.

V.

Home. My eyes were full of tears
as I handed my obol to the ferryman,
my quarter to the woman at the tolls,
and took the last, familiar stretch of road.
There's the all-night donut stand, the endless
chainlink fence bounding the airport field,
there's my favorite beech tree. There at last
our small green townhouse propped between its neighbors.
Oh lighted windows, darkling silhouette
where someone stands against them, waiting to hear
the crunch of gravel and the motor's hush.
So long, so far. I missed you very much.

BACK TROUBLE

And so to bed. My heart is full of poems,
my pillow full of feathers, unexpressed.
Old traveler, what ails you? Misery,
I've traced so many cities on the ceiling.
I couldn't lift my feet today,
much less my faithful suitcase: Amsterdam,
Florence, and Paris waver on the scrim
superimposed by bad, old-fashioned pain.
One vertebra one centimeter crooked,
and sex and plans and jokes and the blue sky
all vanish in a mist.

              Where was I? Lost
in the silvery, self-important old wives' tales
that plaster the television, four days deep
in the puzzling, sad, rhetorical *Confessions*,
where stealing a pear is tantamount,
by Augustine's encompassing calculus
of guilt, to shtupping a woman out of bounds,
torturing armies of eremites, or creating
hell as your crater, if you're a fallen angel.
Drink it all down, you pagans, racked in the flesh!
Out of the scarlet bowl. To your health, to mine.

PILGRIMS

La Coruña is a glazier's heaven,
windowed balconies three stories high
on every housefront, winking at the sea.
We stroll between the ocean's broken mirrors
and their upright, Bauhausian reflections.

Considering the past.
Our past, so discontinuous, with midweek
partings and reunions in the snow.
So many winter dawns you drove away
dutifully, unwillingly, and I
dried my tear and turned to the task at hand.

Each week we closed the difference, over miles
of ice or snow or fog, whatever barred
the miles from Bethlehem to Salamanca,
Bellefonte, Tonawanda, Dubois, Boston.
The long, sad hills of northern Pennsylvania
and New York's southern tier,
strangely reorganized by ancient names.

Each week you took me in your arms again;
we dreamed of Spanish castles.
Really, we dreamed of home. But here we are,
pleased by La Coruña's glittering border,
ready to complete our pilgrimage.

Galicia's green and oceanic hills
roll up on Santiago de Compostela.
Our long midsummer traveling led us here
because in separate, earlier lives we loved
the starred cathedral churches
that map the routes of Europe down to Rome,
distant Jerusalem and Santiago.

The western portals quicken in the burnished
guise of summer evening. Certain chapels
are stained and dazed with mildew, the old plaster
cracks in estuaries, patches of stone
drop like small misfortunes.
But others are designed so ardently
in lunar plateresque, sunburst baroque,
that light is all we see,
and centuries of darkness fall behind.

Self-made, registered pilgrims with their staves
and backpacks circle the plaza. Gypsy children
and hawkers chart their progress carefully,
paying the purse seine out.
So deity long ago collected souls.

This place is not the same that welcomed pilgrims
worldly and devout as Chaucer's kind,
and yet we too have come from far away.
Although we say no prayers,
we watch our votive candles till they fail.

And though we still have miles to go tomorrow,
and still no children and no common home,
today we two accomplished one desire
that waited over years
while we, doubly and singly, bided time
and hoped. However often now our woven
lives converge and separate, my love,
today we've come this far.

72, RUE LEPIC

Beyond our second-story balcony,
foursquare maples and the delicate locust
already spend the first of yellow leaves.
Birds spiral down to splash
in the crusted saucepan doubling as a birdbath,
or the new-fangled sprinkler, when it's on
to keep the roses cool.
Pigeons especially make an amazing flap
in the treetops, heaven shivers, till they fall
plop on the grass with boots and blunderbuss,
a storm of feather-feints that ends in silence.

In general, the quarter's rarely silent.
August workmen bang the walls below
and speculate on girls;
telephones declare from other windows;
garbage rattles down the flue provided;
and cars zoom up the street
or break into alarms when trouble threatens
as it does almost daily, like the rain.

It trails the upward-puffing, earnest tourists
searching for Sacré Coeur by morning light,
and their evening counterparts
hurrying towards the fleshpots of Pigalle.
They pause, discuss their maps, consult the sky,
and then go up or down.
But we stay in the middle, undistracted
by Perigordian domes or hot reviews,
content with the reverie of painted wings
that plays to our borrowed garden,
and gold leaf scattered by an invisible hand
trying to cover the debts of abandoned summer.

BELLEVILLE REVISITED

Enchantment passes, like an afternoon
of sunshine that surprises us
late in a day of cool and rainy weather.
It gleams on my old haunts, the hill of Belleville,
sky-highrises noosing the Place des Fêtes,
the curves of rue Compans, rue de la Mare,
even the rue des Amandiers
that used to house the eighteenth century
inside its little workshops, iterated
courtyards carefully hidden from the street.

We walk together, watching the gutters stream
with briefly lighted refuse, useless silver.
So long ago. How often I returned there,
pulled by love imagined, disappointed
memory, and found and quit again
the life I borrowed sideways in those sorry
neighborhoods. But now I close them down.

No reason anymore to climb
the rue des Solitaires, or circumscribe
the artificial heights of Buttes Chaumont
where rocks are molded concrete, and the faint
vanilla goddess in the air at dawn,
wind shifting from a biscuit factory.

63, RUE MIRABEAU

I.

Not this month, small invisible.
We're waiting. Will you come? Perhaps someday
I'll tell you tales about the house
and garden where we looked for you one summer,
a later day when you have ears and thoughts
and outward vision for imagining
what you have never seen.

Or maybe you'll come back with us
to meet our Paris friends who really live here,
so you can learn the shapes of memory
by pointing. There's my window, see,
where I looked up the hill and wrote
and watched the neighbors' cat pass by
from fence to gate, untrammeled fluency.

Your father's window, on the left-hand side,
looks from the other study through a green
cloud of lilac bush and apple tree,
each with its bird's nest. So he also dreamed.
There's the espaliered pear tree, frailly held
against the wall's desire; when we asked
it counted a dozen pears. (We hope for two.)

Your father knows a bawdy tale
about a lover hidden in a pear tree,
but Chaucer wrote it for another summer.
Dear visible, if you come here someday
I think you'll take your toys and stroll
to a place in the garden neither of your parents
ever saw before, for all their watching.

II.

Let's try our luck again,
crushing the velvet carpet of the grass
as soon as the neighbors vanish for the weekend.
The cat's incursions, or the uncomprehending
choir of pigeons, won't disturb our love.
The lilac boughs will nod as they always do
against the light wind roused
by our disturbances. Small talk, soft talk
lost in the down of leaves.

What are we waiting for? For the world to turn
sleepily on its side,
the heavy sky to fall as rain, and vapor
back in summer's updraft: gray and white
the alternations pass,
border cloud and infinite blue distance
charted occasionally by a passing plane
or the day moon. We're waiting for a change,
our lazy rhythms of embodiment
posing the same question, posing the same
suspenseful, dark, impetuous reply.

Dark Tents and Fires

DARK TENTS AND FIRES

Narrow, encompassing, unsystematic,
those late Victorian houses used to stand
forever against my will.
Ten years ago I said: I want existence
pure as Sartre's or Weil's, hardly a stick
of furniture, and all the world in books.
I sank my souvenirs in hock or storage,
and left the stubborn family walls behind.

Somehow their stones unraveled, over time.
So now my heart returns,
wishful imagining at last embodied
in lamps and tables, dishes, embroidery,
the wrack of my old worlds in Philadelphia.
Worlds are multiple and have their seasons,
it seems, no less materially sketched out
than Bedouin settlements. Dark tents and fires.

How rapidly my generations faded
and left their broken tapestries behind
for me to mend and set in different places,
chairs to refinish, sofas to recover.
I fold the tablecloths and count the spoons,
some of them missing. Where?
Lost in the trash, I fear, anonymously
bent in evening news or toothed disposal.

Lost like my mother's letters, thrown away.
Oh save them! Battered eighteenth-century walls
and fieldstone houses, great white sycamores,
row houses with their porches
facing Delancey, Arch, Spring Garden Streets.
I count and count. The tablecloths are lace,
the napkins linen. Who will wash and press
these remnants, who will polish all the silver?

So many creatures withered from the source,
and only domestic ritual to guard them.
I raise my piecemeal household on the sand
until another wave of emigration
or dust or famine sends us all away
or that day comes, named by a fatal number
not infinite, but passing
my powers of inventory to command.

BOUNDARIES

Behind the hedge of privet, ten feet tall,
was Italy, or all that I imagined:
a white Madonna on a pedestal,
stained glass with olive trees curved in medallions;
and in the graveyard, families and angels
carved in another tongue.
Capelli on the headstones, Serafino
deep in a grove of new world cypresses.
Stone trees with their branches broken in mourning.
Gladiolas tied in grosgrain ribbon
for Domenic, Maria, *padre mio*.

On our side of the hedge, American
and measured off as neighboring backyards,
my friend Angelica Paoli
showed me her martyr-cards,
prayers embellished with a grisly death
on one side, flawless Easter on the other.
She told me there were statues in the church
painted like life and magnified in gold,
Mary holding Jesus holding his heart
as offering to us.
To us? We never asked for such a token.

The lovely, canopied, unclimbable ash
in my backyard was like a pagan chapel;
its crown made even Angelica fall silent.
But really, I was just an Episcopalian
who prayed to God in church

facing a hand-carved rood screen brought from England.
Really, I didn't know if I believed.
And when I left for Italy much later
I stayed so long my father sold the garden
to nameless souls who tore the privet down,
killing our ancient right to boundaries.

SIDONIE

Who's that in the garden? Halfway between
exclusive nature and the world of words.
The garden is a garden because she said
it is, and made it so:
what grows inside its lawful boundaries
is mostly what she thought to carry in,
rosier, laurier, sauge, ficelle de soie
up which the spiraled jut
of blind, light-seeking tendrils take the air.

Except for weeds, and trees already there,
and stones the fertile earth
keeps pushing towards the light, like frozen seeds.
She pries them up, expels them,
or makes them orderly as walls and borders.
Revenants she never entertained
come in by air or passing cat or simply
pop up out of the ground
to change the garden's soft geometry.

Trace of a larger order:
the cat's paw printing a rose
on squares of chocolate drying in the shade.
Aphids in the copper iris, blackfly
graying the lilacs, nettles by the hedges,
and fierce wisteria throttling the bower.
The tired, maternal gardener stands
and sighs, a trowel in one hand, and her silver
scissors, dangling idly, in the other.

TWO PASSAGES FROM COLETTE

I.

The hill smokes with white plum trees,
each one immaterial and dappled
as a round cloud.
At half past five in the morning
under dew and horizontal ray,
the young wheat's unarguably
blue, the earth iron-red,
plum trees copper-pink.
Only for a moment;
the fey dishonest light goes out
with the first hour of day.
Everything grows in godly heat.
The least vegetable creature
hurls itself straight up.
Peonies, blood-red in the first month,
geyser so hard
that stalk and barely unpleated
petals crack, push up, suspend in air
their crust of earth, tipped like a broken roof.

II.

The beak of pruning shears
clacks along the hedge of rose trees.
Another calls back, from the border.
Soon a straw of young sprouts,
tips rosy as dawn,
green and succulent further down,
will lie beneath the roses.
On the border, stiff wands
of apricot, sacrificed,
will burn with small flower-flames
an hour before dying,
and the bees let none of it perish.

SECRET PLACES OF FORREST LANE

Forsythia was a low arcade, a lair
where tendril-branches cast themselves aside
over and over again, gold-studded flowers
in coppery green hair.
A useful place to hide
whenever the fighting hit a certain pitch
or simmered, tight or sober as my father.
My mother did what women usually do
before they draw the line: dissemble, plead,
scold and compensate and throw out bottles.
None of it helps. The drinker has to drown
in his own cups before he comes around,
if he wants to live enough. My father did.

After torrential snows
that flattened the forsythia and dogwood,
after the summer floods that made our lane
a small canal and killed the cellar pump,
after a string of blind catastrophes
that seemed like great adventure to a child
and trouble to my parents,
inspired or terrified, my father quit.

When I crept out of hiding, he was there,
though half-transparent, like an earthly cloud.
Gentle and self-occluded, self-enclosed,
but there. So my young parents ceased to fight
and picked up wiser habits,
inventing my two brothers by surprise.
The township widened Forrest Lane so firmly
the border of forsythia disappeared.
I learned to live without it, now and then
finding my heart a better place to hide.

THE NEOLITHIC REVOLUTION OF 1956

Record snowstorms fell in March, and floods
in August turned the road into a river.
The age of painted cave and totem dream
for me was Forrest Lane
in nineteen-fifty three and four and five.
My family were icons at the center,
fixed among miracles of laundry, rites
of closed or slamming doors,
so many bottles, cigarettes, and quarrels.

And fireflies and picnics and my lamb
who every evening played the same old song
but truly, from the heart.
Beside my bed, the wall was like a garden
scrolled with flowers, borders in between
I traced each night as paths,
blazoned faintly with significant markings
only I could see in the dim light
that drifted through my chamber from the hallway.

Reading put an end to those enchantments.
Sometimes at recess from my first grade labors,
I'd sneak back to the kindergarten room,
a bright, high-windowed place,
open for nothing more than serious playing.
Papier maché and paints and clay and last year's
giant Easter rabbit still in the corner,

and individual letters
that didn't have to bind themselves to words
but stood out all alone, like sounds or colors.

Life not yet arranged in rows of desks
straight as furrows in a field, or streets
that governments can number serially,
or pictograms in columns,
all the neolithic late inventions
that help construct a world
which afterwards the clever, polyglot,
manipulative inventor is bound to live in.
Run, Spot, run. He trails his inky pawprints
across the page, and we,
flush with our powers, chase him out of Eden,
leaving the smoky mysteries and monsters,
the perfect flowers, impossibly behind.

LEGACIES

Aunt Annie said, "When I turned seventeen,
old enough to take the train alone,
I went back to Detroit, and the big house
my father had abandoned, where my mother
Anna Sanger died of scarlet fever
when she was only thirty, eight months pregnant,
trying in vain to carry
his baby to term and leaving three small children.
He shipped us to his mother in the east,
locked the doors behind him, never returned.

"The house was sacked by loose acquaintances,
renters, mice, and brave nocturnal children
who spattered candle wax
on sills of jimmied windows, up the stairs.
All the satin drapes had long since rotted.
Nothing was left but sheet music and letters
(I took them home), the fruit-and-basket love seat
that you and I refinished and revived,
Father's bookshelves with their leaded glass,
handsome but much too heavy to bring back.

"I searched the rooms for traces of my mother,
but found only those polished memories
I'd counted over and over every evening
when I was four, and suddenly far from home.
I know I have her laugh,
and probably her temper. When her brother
came home to die years later, he bequeathed
pawn tickets to us, and a fur he claimed
was hers. Except the monogram was wrong,
and in its empty sleeves, the wrong perfume."

LIFE OF A SALESMAN

Behind the small, fixed windows of the album,
my father sits on sand, flowered with sea-salt,
nestling my younger brothers on his knees,
my mother beside him, me on another towel.

Or else he's smiling, lapped by shallow combers,
holding the kids so only their toes get wet,
free from booze and taxes, the city office,
his territory, miles of empty highway.

My husband, late addition to the family,
points out a disproportion: that generic
photo of my father on the beaches
stands for a man with two weeks' paid vacation.

I say to my brothers, look, you're all contented!
Both of you blue with cold in your ratty towels,
thrilled with the wind, the escalating waves,
our father watching the ocean roll its sevens.

Most of the time, he's on the road again
selling fancy letterhead, engravings
the businessmen he calls on can't be certain
they need, without his powers of persuasion.

He tries to tell them. Fifty weeks a year,
in sun and rain and snow, on secondary
arteries crosshatching the back country
of Pennsylvania, Maryland, West Virginia.

Alone at night in one more shabby diner,
his pale self in the speckled mirror-panels
is like a stranger's. He coats his potatoes
and minute-steak in catsup, for the color.

He wants a drink, but holds off for another
day, another hour. The gray Atlantic
shuffles invisibly. He orders coffee
and maybe calls his sponsor up, long distance.

Or calls my mother next, with lonely questions
she tries to answer, putting on my brothers
who sneeze and whistle, practice words like "daddy"
that touch him at the end of the connection.

The dial tone doesn't sound at all like waves.
He might go to a movie, or a meeting:
there's always one around to fill the shady
dangerous intervals of middle evening.

He likes the coffee's warmth, the sound of voices
circling in on wisdom: know the difference.
Protect him, higher power, when he travels
his hundred miles tomorrow, rain or shine.

His death lies elsewhere, hidden in the future,
far from his wife and children, far away
from cleanly riffled Jersey shores in summer,
the gray Atlantic playing out its hand.

Common Fortune

LETTER TO TOKYO

                        Washington, D.C., September 1985
Dear Eleanor,
                    I happen to be writing
from one of my old haunts, the intersection
of Connecticut with the middle of the second
North West alphabet: Ordway for "O."
The literal organization of this town
goes nicely with its bureaucratic functions.
When I was working here just after college,
the *Post* exposed a government cartel
that made a fortune out of storing paper:
tons of debris in alphabetic files.

What a life that was, planted in Commerce
with thirty thousand other people, bored
to tears and dressed in gray or hot-pink flannel.
I smoked rum-soaked cigars in the elevators,
read the *Post* all morning, hung around
as often as possible in jogging suits,
hit the Mall museums from twelve to three,
and plastered my office walls with Japanese
dragon scrolls, good copies from the Freer.
I lost my nascent interest in politics,

Unlike my roommates, early Nader's Raiders
who worked from dawn to midnight raking muck
around the Capitol in shifty patterns.
We learned to like the system of committees

and twofold Houses, since it breaks up power
and makes the elected talk, but we became
cynical too, in view of all the deals
and double-deals, the sheer stupidity
of office. I departed, but my roommates
stayed for law school, turned Republican.

So here I am on Ordway after the fact
a dozen years. How does it look to you?
Northwest as well, on earth's imagined corner
wherever the blue Pacific meets Japan.
Are you at ease among the dragon-painters,
gardens briefly glimpsed through not impassable
paper walls, and bamboo window frames?
Do their refined, compact accommodations,
their sense of seemly ordering, reveal
anything politic that we could use?

Eleanor, do you think we have a chance
to overshadow the phantoms of destruction
invented about the time that we were born?
How can our talkative poems come to bear
against the ghostly silences? They must,
since virtue's only virtuous when it acts
and most of acting's speaking. Shall we say,
my friend, that dragons are a happy omen?
That we revise our monsters into allies,
our bitterest wars of speech, to making worlds?

We go on tithing, signing the next petition,
trying just to oppose more obvious kinds
of evil-hour obtuseness, hoping the wave
that carries us on has other, similar droplets;
and yet the extrapolation's hard to trust.
I think of you en route with your green suitcase
packed with strophes, stratagems, painted dragons,
and send this letter after you, northwest,
straight from the heart of government that falters,
skips a beat, begins and beats again.

SYMMETRY

I've cleared myself a place at a wooden table
crowded with books and papers,
work suspended by my friend the poet
while he and his family summer in the Marches.
The library's quiet, backwards-looking window
gazes onto the rise of Butte Montmartre,
now lined by sober grillwork
and framed by ancient, velvet, pale mauve curtains.
Facing me, a cupboard stacked with offprints
written by my host tilts gently sideways.

But I'm uncertain, writing where I sit
and browsing carefully through all these books,
searching for what? A poet and a woman,
I find my culture strange,
when overwhelmingly the musing agent
turns out to be a man, and in the wings,
the muted, busy companion is a woman
keeping the children quiet
or bravely imitating a bowl of fruit.

I spent two hours this morning cleaning house.
Bonnard was already in his studio, painting,
Morandi too (Giacometti was still asleep).
Marthe was doing the laundry, wondering
perhaps if they'd ever marry.
Morandi's three devoted, charming sisters
were bargaining at the market
under the fair arcades of *Bologna Grassa*.
Alberto's girl had long since hit the streets;
his mother, in Switzerland, was weeding flowers.

Bonnard's nudes are almost always Marthe,
but the plaques say only *Nue*,
a naked woman, a cloud, moving and silent.
Visitors will praise Morandi's sisters
for their table's vivacity,
pleasing talk, and raft of Egyptian spices,
but fail to recall their names.
And who could list the girls of Giacometti?
Certainly not his mother,
also anonymous and caught like them
in the fine, distorted nets of his gray pencil.

The world of culture slants away from me,
I fit its shelves and don't. Whom should I speak for?
Those wives and maids and models
used to speak for themselves sharply enough
in the case of an ailing child or a boney chicken
or beauty's indecent tariff;
although they are silent now,
and never devised a poem or drew a face.
They sang, or sketched a symmetry on paper
that someone used as tinder the next day.
So lately I suppose
I have to weave two lines in all I say:
recorded tenor, evanescent alto;
fixed trellis, quick and immemorial vine.

ATHENS BUS STATION

For Eleni

Waiting side by side at little tables,
crowded on benches, sweltering
in August's unrelenting density,
we drink our lemon sodas, hum along
to songs by Hadzidakis, aural ghosts
who haunt the ear and, in that roaring hall,
the radio.

What was I thinking of?
A small white house in sunlight,
wild orchids on the table, Parian honey,
speckled eggs, a stew of amber figs,
and one bluebottle fly that never settles.

Arleta's fluting voice drifts down the hall
where we sit quietly among our friends,
suitcases, children, swept by clouds of diesel.

Forgetfulness, she sings. But we
remember lemon trees blooming in April,
then ripening, beneath their roof of leaves,
small planets on the layered eave of twilight.

LETTERS FROM PARIS

April 5, 1974

Dear Emily,
               This letter's overdue;
I wanted to write you many times last winter,
but somehow life enforced my isolation.
I've got to come home soon. My mother wonders
how her own daughter and red diaper baby
could emigrate, when so much work remains
for all of us at home.
I still believe America's the only
place I have a chance to really change things.
This life is almost over; I have to leave,
but need a little time to catch my breath,
or stoke my courage. One day I'll decide,
mail all my books by surface, pack a suitcase.
Go. After a while, when spring is over.

Mostly I'm staying out in Auteuil with Yves
and his two little girls. It's strange to live,
almost, with a rich doctor in the suburbs.
Suddenly I've acquired a house and children,
cats, a long walled garden.
Thursdays and Saturdays I imitate
a bourgeois matron setting off for market
armed with expanding string-bags, like a fish net:
my catch is cauliflower, country bread,
radishes, Normandy butter, liters of wine.
The girls come home from school and we eat lunch

together in the garden, where the sun
translates itself behind the lilac bushes
before it starts its afternoon decline.

Whenever Bernard comes over for the evening
and brings his charming instruments, alive,
almost, with paws and tails and nacreous eyes,
and some of our old crowd from Père Lachaise,
then I feel more at home.
We settle in, tune up, and then make music
just like old times in the small atelier
on rue des Amandiers. Caught in the spell
of coolly amorous, melancholy measures,
Yves forgets the hospital, and I
forget my term of exile, my confusions.

May Day 1974

Dear Emily,
        Don't worry, I'm okay.
The days when I go over to Vincennes
I feel more confident, more like myself,
at least, more certain of my own first causes.
I'm finishing my *license* in Chinese
by two night courses I enjoy immensely,
although their combination baffles me.
One night we read the poetry of Tu Fu
and Li Po, character by character,
each syllable, it seems, tagged by a gloss

of pages. But I like those gentlemen,
courteous, drunken, exiled.
The other night we simply read the papers,
talk about modern China in Chinese.
Two worlds, Emily. I suppose they fit
together in some oriental puzzle,
except for me it's still scattered in pieces.
I ought to visit China too, someday.

The students at Vincennes are mostly older,
busy with children and their daytime work.
My favorite classmate's a Vietnamese doctor
who wants to go to China soon, to learn
the other half of earthly medicine.
Once in a while she asks me home for supper
and we talk politics; her eldest son
studies quietly in another room.
Where are her other children?
After I leave her house, my vision swims
with images of war, and my ears burn
with fragments of four languages, at odds.

I'd like to invite her back for dinner too,
but hesitate because, you know, she studied
with Yve's Françoise the year before she died.
I even met her here on one occasion
when Chinese students visited the house,
and Françoise still was able to entertain

and teach. The garden was lit with paper lanterns
and Chinese people playing vehement ping-pong.
The girls were toddlers, climbing on their mother
who sat in an armchair, pale but animated,
telling students about her own impressions
of China, where she studied in the sixties.
It was, she often said, the happiest,
hardest, and simplest period of her life.
Yves and I fixed dinner,
and absentmindedly burnt up the rice.

May 29, 1974

Dear Emily,
            I'll put this in the mail
as soon as it stops raining. (Don't believe
those stories about Paris in the spring.)
Last night as I was driving to Vincennes,
I dropped in early at the atelier
near Père Lachaise. Bernard was cooking stew
and had already, of course, uncorked a bottle,
so we sat down to dinner. He's immersed
in Malcolm Lowry's *Under the Volcano*,
but full of gossip. Malice keeps him happy,
and everyone we know is grist for stories.
He left the old apartment,
bought himself a mattress, sink, and stove,
and simply lives behind the atelier.

He's not entirely lonely, not so old,
except his teeth are bad. Ten years ago
he used to earn his living playing jazz.
Then he started losing
his teeth and, naturally, his embouchure.
That's when he built his first viola da gamba,
a painted harpsichord soon afterwards
for well-heeled clients. Last night after supper
I sat there quietly for half an hour
in rosy wine-clouds, watching the studio;
and missed already those half-animate
animal instruments, the polished goose necks,
inlaid ivory and feathered bellies,
scales of rosewood, hand-carved dragon tails.

This life that holds me, gradually releases.
Bernard just let me sit there with my thoughts;
he played a tape, Scarlatti, washed the dishes,
and then began some process in the corner
of sanding down, refining wood to satin.
At last I left for class.
I said *adieu* instead of *au revoir*,
and watched him stand a moment in the doorway,
shadows on a patch of parchment gold.
Good-bye, good-bye. I'm writing you this letter
perhaps so I can honestly tell someone
hello, I'll see you soon. Look for me.

Laurie

LETTER FROM TORONTO

Toronto
April 15, 1989

Dear Hudson Review,

I had lunch today at the Art Gallery of Ontario, with two invisible women for whose sake I had visited the gallery in the first place. My aunt Janette Pierce died unexpectedly of a heart attack at the age of fifty-seven about a year ago, and my friend Dorothy Roberts (whose poetry you have regularly published since the mid-fifties) lives three hundred miles south and is unable to travel now. My brief tenure at the University of Toronto where I have been a research fellow this year is drawing to a close; I'm preparing to say good-bye to the admirable library system and the jet-black squirrels that scamper around Queen's Crescent. But my sojourn here has been so consistently colored by thoughts of my aunt and of Dorothy that I felt in need of a ceremonious leave-taking that included them.

So I'm sitting in the elegant Member's Lounge of the AGO, drinking a cup of coffee and writing away on the back of long white order forms. Dorothy and Aunt Jane quite enjoy each other's company, so I can gracefully drop out of the conversation for a while; they're discussing the sculptural, totemic paintings of Emily Carr. Both are articulate, animated, and possessed of a delightful sense of humor; Aunt Jane is wearing a pair of her famous three-dollar earrings, and Dorothy one of her lovely brooches. My aunt keeps posing questions with a journalist's intensity; Dorothy counters with a poet's unexpected insight, and her long familiarity with the cultural life of Canada. (They talked this way on the one occasion they actually met.) Writers themselves, they don't mind if I sit and scribble.

My first trip to Toronto occurred in virtue of Aunt Jane. She was a staff member (and finally editor) of the *Episcopalian,* national paper of the American Episcopal Church. Since she traveled a great deal in connection with her reportorial duties and worked very hard, she was careful about how she spent her vacation time. Usually she went camping in one of the beautiful, underutilized state parks of northwest Pennsylvania or drove up to Stratford, Ontario for the Shakespeare Festival with a small subset of her seven children. But one summer about five years ago when I was in the doldrums, she kindly picked me up at Penn State on her way north from Philadelphia, and proposed to show me a bit of Canada.

Various adventures ensued: torrential rainstorms, a midnight visit to Niagara Falls illuminated not by the moon but by lime-green spotlights, a pageant at an Indian reservation we were too sad to watch and fled, dead fish and fancy pebbles at the edge of Lake Huron, the purchase of an astonishing Chinese smoking jacket in an antique store, Shakespeare and swans at Stratford. Wherever we went in Ontario, she was reminded of passages from the novels of Robertson Davies, whose strange blend of locally colored realism and magic she tried to describe, to my puzzlement. But the high point of the trip was our visit to the AGO in Toronto, where my aunt displayed an unsuspected wealth of knowledge about Canadian painting. She was a wonderful tourist; she never went anywhere, even on business, without learning something substantial about the world she passed through. Relations with the Anglican Church of Canada had often brought her to Toronto, where she discovered the "Group of Seven," and to Vancouver, where she discovered Emily Carr.

Back at Penn State, I took her to visit Dorothy, who also

suddenly proved quite knowledgeable about Canadian painting, under the astute questioning of my aunt. I'd realized that Dorothy's brother Goodridge was a well-respected painter of the last generation, but never was able to put him in context. As Dorothy produced books and catalogs from hitherto unexplored shelves and corners, I started to see how early-twentieth-century Canadian painters learned to exploit their formal debt to European painting, the decorative arabesques of *Jugendstil* and the expansive colorism of the Impressionists, without succumbing to its imperious example.

The Group of Seven in particular did so by bringing their painterly skills to bear on a new subject matter: the wilderness around Georgian Bay, Algonquin Park and the north shore of Lake Superior. They became campers, hikers, and canoeists, environmentalists *avant la lettre,* through the great aesthetic (and nationalist) experiment that produced the most important of their works. Truly, the harsh sublimity of those northern woods and lakes, in combination with the courage and generosity of the painters' response to it, produced unprecedented, monumental painting. (And I have felt a similar selflessness and transport in Dorothy's nature poetry, though her poems belong to the hills and woodlands of New Brunswick.)

On my next birthday, Davies's *Deptford Trilogy* arrived from my aunt, and I lived inside them, enthralled, for a fortnight, finally understanding what she'd meant to say about them the summer before. Later, during my very last conversation with her, I mentioned I'd decided to spend this year at the University of Toronto. A week or so afterwards, she had died; when my husband and I returned home from her funeral, we found in the mail our belated Christmas present: guest membership at the AGO, offered with love from Jane. Each month when I get their newsletter (which I sometimes pass on to Dorothy) I feel as if I'm receiving belated news from my aunt. The correspondence is rather one-way; I want to write back, to tell her that I've got a room in Massey College where Robertson Davies was master and still maintains an office. I haven't actually encountered him, but I see his severe, level-eyed bust at the corner of the library stairs every time I descend to use the public telephones. And whenever I walk through the courtyard I think, with a blend of local realism and magic, that I might see him stroll by in his long white beard.

So today I went back to the AGO, to renew our membership, see my favorite paintings again, and pass a quiet moment, remembering. The permanent installation of the Group of Seven has recently been reorganized, and is now even more inviting and easy to navigate. Coming up the stairs to the second floor, I was immediately struck by a landscape of Goodridge Roberts's I hadn't seen before: "Georgian Bay" (1952). Roberts seems to have eschewed the decorative aspects of his predecessors' work; this view of Georgian Bay is studiedly random and unadorned. The nervous brushwork of trees and water in the middle ground is balanced against a deep blue, pacific sky. In the foreground, brush and rubble strewn on bare earth look almost calligraphic. Two smaller oils of his, "Hills and Rivers, Laurentians" and "Small Bridge and Rapids" (both from 1940), are displayed in the first gallery next to work of his most distinguished contemporaries, including Emily Carr. Four stunning oils by Carr are hung side by side on a facing wall, views of Indian villages, which, with their haunting totems and ritual imagery, would be reminiscent of Gauguin if Carr's handling of contours and her reduced but intense coloration of foliage and sky were not so strongly idiosyncratic.

The next gallery houses the Group of Seven exhibit. Included as well are paintings by Tom Thomson, who died too

Tom Thomson
THE WEST WIND (1917)
Oil on canvas

Courtesy: Art Gallery of Ontario
Gift of the Canadian Club of Toronto,
1926

early (drowned in a canoeing accident) to be officially included in the group, although he exercised a profound influence on all of them. The exhibit culminates in three large, magnificent landscapes, hung together on the same wall, filling the room with the enigmatic pathos of nature untouched by rural or urban reconstruction, and yet surrendered to the human eye. On the right is Lawren Harris's "Above Lake Superior" (1922), in which half a dozen trees, denuded by forest fire, stand before a somber hill and cloud-striated sky. The cylindrical forms of tree and cloud recall Leger, but the gaping, stripped, and yet wholly successful composition, and the breathing mortality of the landscape, are Harris's invention. On the right is J. E. H. MacDonald's "Fall, Montreal River" (1920), a dynamic, shining view of rapids winding among hills.

In the center stands the painting I love the most, whose radiantly muted colors no reproduction can ever capture. Like the Titians I go back and back to in Europe, this painting demands regular pilgrimages and never fails to enchant me with each apparition. It is Tom Thomson's "The West Wind" (1916–17). Study of *Jugendstil* decoration surely taught him how to handle the simplified and alluring curves of a group of wind-stunted pine trees in the foreground, and Impressionism inspired the mottled sky and water behind. But the combination of stylized linearity and impressionist light-play is utterly novel, and the stressed distortion of the trees, the wildness of water were his own discovery in the face of a fatally compelling nature that would very soon claim his life. Growing out of a shore of invented purple, green, red, and ochre, the trees form a sort of rood screen that organizes and includes the chaos of turbulent water and air, savage divinities rising up behind them.

So I sat and mused, and then walked over to get lunch, and take up the conversation with my invisible companions. How

odd friendship is, that continues in spite of immediate and end-
less absences. Two women often guided me around Toronto,
though one was indisposed at home, and the other was gone.
Aunt Jane assured me that she still has an address, though I
won't be able to write it down. Dorothy reminded me of the
last stanza in her poem "Dazzle," that praises the truth of
appearances, the interchange of light and shadow:

> Light plays with the chorus of the living
> While the dead hurry down
> Earthward to lift to the dazzle
> Any answering form.

A POEM FOR POLLY

Hazel eyes, light voice, a stubborn jaw,
honey-colored hair, quick moderate gestures,
the natural athelete's physical impatience:
clearly, in my dream the friend I walked with
arm-in-arm, was you. Still unconsoled,
you wanted a poem fit to settle questions
I knew I couldn't answer.
Who can explain the destiny of children
that hardens into drama as they grow?

Nothing occurs but detail.
We went to scouts and chorus and the movies,
shaping the world by gossip, eating cookies
equally shaped by our small reckless hands.
We babysat on weekends, stayed up late
and scared ourselves by watching Twilight Zone,
or went to dancing classes
decked out like little madam butterflies
and scared the boys with our intense illusions.

Sport was your talisman.
We joined the local swimming club; you headed
for varsity and won, and then went on
to pick up tennis too, hockey and soccer.
I think of you with something in your hand,
a ball, a towel, a racket, leaping up
beautifully to connect trajectories,

at home in all the elements but fire.
I wonder if you made it through the fire,

the one that stokes the last sublunar sphere,
or Dante's Purgatory. Where you are
is hard to say, and yet hard not to say.
Dear pretty blonde, you learned so easily
the skills of those who dress themselves in white
for tea or tennis, your success obscured
how bitterly you aimed at some perfection
no one attains down here
where all of us have freckles, flaws, and scars.

Gray hairs and wrinkles now, if you could see.
At seventeen, you gradually went mad,
divided as two incommensurate girls,
the model Sunday schooler, and the bad one
who ran away from home and smoked cigars
and dope and even, I think, put out for boys.
You had two different voices, and you wept
only in Bad; in Good, your eyes were bright
and hopeless, like a doll's.

"She's such a doll." You were, close to the end,
fragile and artificial, your hair dyed
platinum to imitate pure blondness
instead of the mixed-up brown and gold it was.

You left your friends behind, and ran around
in Main Line circles: snobs and featherdusters
swallowed your parents' booze and canapés
and laughed at you behind your back. You knew.
I know you raised a cup for old acquaintance,
your everyday lost life, but you were out
too far, the tide was running, you were cold.

Three months of college must have left you tired
and wilder still. At Christmas I expected
your call that never came. Instead you climbed
out of your parents' house one frozen night
to watch the stars, or worse, up on the roof.
Beside yourself, you faltered where you stood
and then let go and slid the whole way down
and broke. Your adequate, ingenuous
small frame dismissed itself
as perfect snowflakes smoothed it in the dark,
first melting and then resting, ice to ice.

ELEGY

Williamsville, May 1988

Dear Michael Jasper,

                    After a cold, wet April,
spring has finally come to our piecemeal village
stashed between highways, train tracks, airport fields.
Its boundaries are straight, but the vagrant stream
that puzzles local residents slips through town
in a series of crescents, falls, and sliding fans.
So I take streamside walks, avoid the roads,
and think of you sometimes, meandering.

The season's rich, small boy: grape hyacinth
and lily of the valley burden the grass;
musical aunts in the family of roses,
apple and pear, play intricate variations
on amber and white, on cinnamon, honey, cream;
the maples cover themselves with coral flowers
and rush into leaf; the lilacs are almost ready
with clusters of folded incense, hearts for leaves.

Dear heart, green sprout, you'll miss this overripe
extravagant wide spring, the very season
most of us savor and visit in memory
to comfort the griefs of summer, winter's zero.
But all you know is autumn's fading gold.
Leaving us, you crossed the seasons' senses,
sowing the fall with elements of spring
and now in seed-time, memories of snow.

GIFTS

For Jamie and Kathy

Midwifery's lore prescribes
tennis balls as balm
for back labor. If the baby's
head presses the spine
hard in passing, a ball or so
(wrapped in a clean white sock)
can serve as counter-pressure
to override the pain.

So summers in mid-Vermont,
quiet, measured, green,
provide two of my friends
with balm for the talkative,
sub-zero Chicago winter.
They sparked their firstborn there,
nine months later homing
east to bring him forth.

Talk in Chicago is bracing;
Vermont's silences pall;
the overall balance is just.
The only sadness about
their two-world arrangement
is closing the house in August
and leaving the country dog
Blue, on winter board.

Blue waits from September
to May, as patiently
as robins wait for spring.
Without fail, he recalls
their footfall and bounds out
to greet their sure return,
as robins greet the wayward,
inevitable west wind.

My friends can always tell how
ungrudgingly forgiven
they are, by Blue's gift-giving.
He brings them mice, apples,
turtles, and one pained
silver night of nights,
as they hurried to the car,
two faded tennis balls.

WAITING FOR NEWS OF JACKIE'S FIRSTBORN

Your mother gave you a romantic name,
dreams of erotic transport, opera lessons.
Mine named me for a beloved maiden aunt
and took me around to outlets for my dresses.
We loved our mothers, and we loved each other
despite our mothers' mutual distrust.
Not enough stylish brio. Not enough
tough intellectuality. They judged
their daughters too, and so we judged ourselves.

And since we dreamed the ratio parent:child
in terms of mother:daughter, it now seems
doubly riddling that you'll get a son,
as all the silvery sonograms foretell,
that I so far have only begotten lines
of argument and poems. Where's the girl
we thought would clarify our married lives
and long divisions? Somehow you and I
must come to common fortune by ourselves.

LETTER FROM IVRY

July 1987

Dear François and Françoise,

I'm writing by the window of Françoise's study
that looks out over rising green today.
I like the streets and half-streets climbing the hill
behind your house: garages, two-room houses,
kitchen gardens, walls propped behind walls.
By glimpses only, I guess them from the window,
or spy as I wander up to the marketplace
through slatted verges, hedges, and lattices.
A fleet of cats drifts through this neighborhood,
hostile but curious, their amber eyes
fixed on a certain end, their bodies curved
with the converse torsion of means. Indecorous dogs
spray their territorial marks on the housefronts,
scatter them over the sidewalks, bay in the lapse
of radio waves and the ring-road's tidal roar.
Swallows, I think, live over the crest of the hill;
we see their silhouettes in high, bright circles,
but they seldom settle here in the shaggy ivy
that covers the wall next door, and the gaping roof
the landlord stripped to the rafters tile by tile
in a final desperate measure to evict
that genial ruffian who paid him the rent
like an oyster-eater (skipping the months with "r")
and got into brawls in each of the tiny half-dozen
bar-cafés along rue Mirabeau.

Maybe your guests can leave this place you live in
renovated by a fresh perspective.
Your house on the charming, almost gothic arch
of Mirabeau is fitted in like a keystone
carved with the emblems of domestic life.
Two boxes of immortal pink petunias,
perched in spite of occasional blossom theft
at street level on the outside window ledges,
bloom and bloom, indifferent to the weather.
Whenever I open the tall, lace-curtained windows
to water them, I'm always tempted to baptise
the passers-by if they look in need of a drink
or resurrection, as they often do.
Yet somehow I refrain. Because of the flowers,
your house confronts the street with open hands;
because of the lace curtains and hidden garden,
it also gently protects its privacies.
We're grateful for the wealth you keep inside.
The studies are full of books, so is the stairwell
and everywhere else a shelf could be fitted in,
even over the stove in the half-pint kitchen.
Lightly imprinted by the valentines
of lilac leaves, and arabesques of clouds,
the rooms retain the echo of children's voices.
Thank you. We've been happy in this house.

Flower, Sailboat, Child

LISTENING

Words in my ear, and someone still unseen
not yet quite viable, but quietly
astir inside my body;

not yet quite named, and yet
I weave a birthplace for him out of words.

Part of the world persists
distinct from what we say, but part will stay
only if we keep talking: only speech
can re-create the gardens of the world.

Not the rose itself,
but the School of Night assembled at its side
arguing, praising, whom we now recall.

A rose can sow its seed
alone, but poets need their auditors
and mothers need their language for a cradle.

My son still on his stalk
rides between the silence of the flowers
and conversation offered by his parents,
wise and foolish talk, to draw him out.

THIRTY-SIX WEEKS

Ringed like a tree or planet, I've begun
to feel encompassing,
and so must seem to my inhabitant
who wakes and sleeps in me, and has his being,
who'd like to go out walking after supper
although he never leaves the dining room,
timid, insouciant, dancing on the ceiling.

I'm his roof, his walls, his musty cellar
lined with untapped bottles of blue wine.
His beach, his seashell combers
tuned to the minor tides of my placenta,
wound in the single chamber of my whorl.
His park, a veiny meadow
plumped and watered for his ruminations,
a friendly climate, sun and rain combined
in one warm season underneath my heart.

Beyond my infinite dark sphere of flesh
and fluid, he can hear two voices talking:
his mother's alto and his father's tenor
aligned in conversation.
Two distant voices, singing beyond the pillars
of his archaic mediterranean,
reminding him to dream
the emerald outness of a brave new world.

Sail, little craft, at your appointed hour,
your head the prow, your lungs the sails
and engine, belly the sea-worthy hold,
and see me face to face:
No world, no palace, no Egyptian goddess
starred over heaven's poles,
only your pale, impatient, opened mother
reaching to touch you after the long wait.

Only one of two, beside your father,
speaking a language soon to be your own.
And strangely, brightly clouding out behind us,
at last you'll recognize
the greater earth you used to take me for,
ocean of air and orbit of the skies.

AUTUMN SONATA

The ducks are raucous, flying overhead,
and all the talk you hear is running slower.
You don't quite get the words,

not yet, but you can estimate the music.
Anger makes you weep, and a good laugh
raises your toothless smile.

You stand to look, and listen as you sit
in the laps of people talking,
wondering what the tides of life can carry.

Your hair is soft as milkweed;
your father and I caress your head
whenever we hold you, half unthinkingly,

and you move up against that stroking hand.
Your body curves along us when you're full
and arches when you're hungry.

We speak to you by name
and you look sideways, willing but mystified,
trying hard to grasp at dancing straws,

to sing, to show, to answer, to remember
one by one the grape leaves as they tumble,
somber oak and yellow jewelweed.

And yet, for the most part, you soon forget.
And so I write this down
so you can tell us later what it means.

My voluble, mute son,
who listen as the birds go storming south,
you know the melody, but not the words.

ROMANCE

Bound to my computer downstairs, I hear
strange music floating on another floor:
Himalayan folksongs, and the signature
love plaint from the latest Hindi movie.
And in between, the baby's silver laughter.
When can I stop for lunch? Our habits change
with yak cheese in the kitchen.
Now our lunch is rice with curried beans
and salty tea that tastes like chicken soup
whipped to froth with a forked hazel wand.

Balancing rice on a spoon in the wrong hand,
I nurse the boy while Thinley tells us stories
of life caught in the mountains.
Tales of ghosts and fairies, not inventions
but sober resurrection of her facts:
the child who talked to ravens, the shamaness
who cures her clients with a bloodless dagger,
the wife whose passion burned her to a leaf.

Even in this college town, she keeps
the shadowy romance of her native country
double-woven through the warp of days.
Her husband serves the king by studying
western administration; her confidante's
an almost exiled princess
who gravely traded us a royal blue
Tibetan carpet for mere yankee dollars.

Now it's where the baby likes to practice
his offices of hand and eye: he throws
his rattle down on webs of holy scarves
and swords out of their scabbards. *Come and play!*
Our son, it seems, is wise beyond his days;
he set our hearts on Thinley
when we went out to interview, and so
brought magic to the house and the long shadow,
jagged, fantastic, of the Himalayan rim,
and music falling like a mountain wind.

THE OUTDOOR MARKET AT CASSIS

Forty roses wrapped in cellophane,
tied with purple ribbon. Goat cheese, speckled,
redolent, moldy, squared in chestnut leaves.
Kalamata olives soaked in garlic.

Ivory gladiolas bound in sheaves.
Raspberries set like garnets, apricots
displayed on grape leaves, golden *pommes reinettes*
modestly wrapped, a blush on either cheek.

Thyme sprigs, lavender soap, dry artichoke flowers,
statice, poppies, gypsies, children, dogs.
Wary Africans selling belts and statues.
Peasants watching over small potatoes.

Silvery sea-trout laid on marble slabs
like miniature king salmon. Clicking crabs,
dog-faced rascasse slapping out of breath.
Shining, trembling eels, short-circuited.

THE SAILBOAT

Last night, a beautiful boat entered the harbor.
We watched it tack from hills outside of town
where our fifth-floor balcony
dominates an escalade of roofs
and the fish-wife's quiet garden.
Somber, but light still faded in the sky.
The boat was teak or rosewood, sleek, three-masted,
strung from stem to stern with colored lights;
its passengers waited on deck to come ashore
in a fleet of bobbing rowboats.

We both stood up from dinner, torn, excited,
not knowing what to do.
Tourists and townsfolk crowded on the jetty
to welcome the apparition
as if it were a ship of the Phaeacians,
Homer's living *factum*, swifter than thought,
a rosewood dolphin straying in the harbor.
We coaxed the baby to sleep, and then made love.
At three, it was still alight, riding at anchor.
This morning, it was gone.

Only the fishing boats were out, the ragtag
mites of the sailing school and the hobbled craft
that ferry tourists around.
Romance fades with daybreak anyway.
Foreigners wake to find their wallets gone,
their windshields shattered, wine

turned to vinegar in their hearts and kidneys.
Townsmen ring up stock and count their proceeds
by shadowy registers, blind
to the vast light always changing on the headlands.

And when we come down later for our coffee
and paper, we only hear
that last night's elfin host
were drunk and mortal friends of the tire magnate
who owns the promontory,
off-limits with its castle and ruined fortress.
They've all gone off to Nice for another round
of rich and famous lifestyles, on this azure
coast where each of us, the high or middling,
hopes for a second taste of paradise.

EXCURSION TO THE THIRD *CALANQUE*

The third and deepest fiord, furthest from town,
has canyon walls that rise two hundred meters,
raked white limestone pocketed with pine
and broom. So finely hidden,
so hard to reach on foot, the shallow beach
at the *calanque*'s sharp narrowing is silent.
No better place to slip
the overpopulation of Cassis;
blare of cars, and motorboats' excrescence
vanish altogether into the hush
of waves on sand. The ribbed, distended water
is wholly clear, pushed clean by hidden springs.

We didn't walk in overland. I'm scared
or careful about carrying the baby
on gravel-covered tracks that mount straight up,
then tumble from pine to pine
exuberant, crooked, headlong to the water.
We floated in by tourist motorboat,
its engines cut to a purr, the company quiet.
Our mate and captain dropped their explanations
and sat for a moment, watching:
Two old fishermen, tired of fighting the sea,
yet somehow not content with their present catch
of foreigners, Parisians, Marseillais.

Wind in the pines, waves on the lucid shore,
the fading archaic languages of earth.
Our translators knew enough
to keep it to themselves. The baby slept
with milk on his cheek, the run of his vocables
doused in the fortunate rocking of the sea.
But once we entered open water again,
the mate observed, his wishes
lingering still on what we left behind,
"Can't stay too long in heaven." *No, don't say it,*
I thought, and the baby turned
fretfully to my breast, and cried in his dream.

RAIN OR SHINE

The squall is over. Clouds have swept away
their own long overtones and colors deepen
across the seascape: purple, turquoise, plum-green, high above
where the cliff rises, slanting rose and ochre.
The school for sailboats ventures out again,
a line of willful flower-sails that breaks
and wanders from instruction, reconvenes,
and puffs back into shore.

My pot of lavender on the balcony
keeps blossoming, and rustles in the wind
that rises like a question afterwards.
A weather helicopter skirts the cape,
transmitting part of the answer I can see
with my own eyes to all the inland watchers:
"Clouds drift down the coast
to Monaco. Dream of a cool but sunny weekend."

Shelley wouldn't have stayed here. It's too cold
and changeable for a delicate *souffrant.*
Whitecaps on the sea, the mistral blowing
every other day, hardly a palm tree
flourishing anywhere, except in hotel baskets.
Only a year ago
winter frost brought down the eucalyptus
all over town, and left the apartments bald.

The baby's in a sweater, pants, and socks,
though he won't wear a hat. Half-potentate,
half-prisoner, he went off in the stroller
pushed by his musing father
whose pockets are full of tax returns and letters home.
Our letters tend to ramble; we're getting tired,
a little, of our long term in paradise
where no one speaks the language.

Don't want to live forever.
Don't want to climb the mountain, sail away
to Africa, fly high in a weather plane,
hop a freight to Paris.
Just want to rock my baby on my knee,
nurse him when he's hungry, wait and see
the shape of blue that opens up between two clouds:
the boy's light silver and his father's gold.

DREAM-TREE AND MOON

A cypress tree outside the kitchen window
left open for a cross-breeze, smoulders.
Curls of incense mystify the air
still warm two or three hours past midnight.
That's the scent of my lost youth, dispelled.
It woke me up. So wide awake, so tired,
my dreams have cracked a little.

Child and husband sleep in the next room.
The sea moves quietly beneath our terrace,
carries the low complaint of fishermen
casting off in the boats.
They're all as old as I am, forty, older.
The trade is dying out: they fish too hard,
hold back too many fingerlings, their tithe.

Two disparate silvers — streetlamp, crescent moon —
cross the deserted streets.
They cover the tree of dreams, the doorway
back to the crowded bed
where my dear counterparts lie fast asleep.
There's no alternative
beside the one I love.

How quietly the cypress sifts its darker
aromatic shadow. No one hears
except a wakeful mother, caught
in the unawaited trammels of middle age.
Except a few old fishermen
out to fathom the sometimes peaceful sea
for its elusive children. Except the moon
that shivers, blends, absorbs
the lower strata of our human lights.

THE POT OF BASIL

I stripped my office walls of travel posters,
memorabilia, maps, the great charade
of gateways to the world,
all the exotic places I'd rather be.
I threw out the Greek wine
long turned to vinegar in its plastic bottle,
lavender emollient, silk fisherman's line,
invitations to openings in Florence.
The wishing-windows closed,
my office is only a cubicle full of books.

Nowhere I'd rather be than where I am
now that my life has circled back again,
but home, a mile away
where my small boy's just rounding the great horn
of dreams: da Gama, Byrd, Odysseus.
Waking up to the world at every moment,
he navigates the house from chair to chair
ahead of us all and full of stratagems.

Benjamin, whenever I sit with you
looking up and dancing on my knees,
or sleeping on my shoulder, heart to heart,
your steady breathing weight
becomes the certain measure of my life,
center round which the cracked sphere of stars
can turn, as once earth's humbler citizens
flocked about Orpheus.

With you fast in my arms,
I'm back again in the heart's Italy,
safe on a terraced hillside facing east
across the pensive Mediterranean.
Sailboats pause beyond us, close below
fishermen gather nets on the shore to dry.
Oleander glitters in the hedges
and wind dispenses lavender and thyme,

Indefinitely. Content,
we gaze across the coruscating carpet
that stretches out to Poros and a pot
of basil in the kitchen window, greening
in occasional winter sun.
My office shrinks and swells; it's time to go
home to the little boy who waits for me.
How much distance does a life require?
Since you sailed in lately out of nowhere,
we trace our pleasures in a finer pattern
of waking, eating, playing,
pool and splash of sunbeams on the floor.

PROPORTIONS OF THE HEART

In classical flower arrangement,
Masako says, three major stems occur.
The *shin* stands thirty degrees from vertical.
The *soë*, forty-five degrees,
is just three-quarters of the *shin* in height.
The *hikaë*, three-quarters of the *soë*,
points outwards, low, at seventy-five degrees;
most often this one is a flower.

What a classicist I have become,
impelled by the broad hand of revelation,
that is, experience.
Masako's creatures fill our country house
like novel theorems from the *Elements;*
out of fixed proportion, beauty rises
unlike any that I used to summon
in rented rooms from floppy big bouquets.

A single sweep of branch, unflowering,
another upward twist,
and there's the shape of nothing caught in air,
somehow the proper counterpart of one
or two explosive flowers.
Don't be afraid, she says, her fingers hidden
inside the vase, to put more details in,
as long as they don't interrupt the lines.

The heart's most elegant, extravagant
designs arise, I see,
from careful choice and rapid computation.
In half an afternoon, Masako fills
our baskets large and small, and the clear vases.
Two leans from one, and three from one and two,
and suddenly altogether they compose
their ratios to self-sufficiency.

Even the purple brambles in the field,
cut by Masako, fall in whole ellipses,
and twigs repeat their angles on the branch.
So may you and I and our small flower
flourish in the constraints
space and number pose on families;
and make our tracery around the center
of certain loss more beautiful, and sure.

THE SHAPE OF DESIRE

Tracing an airplane's pale trajectory,
you always point, and finish, "Airplane *gone.*"
Waking from dreams about your babysitter's
dark-eyed, clever daughter, you conclude,
"Lulu *gone,*" and hurry to the door's
long windowpane to see her reappear
freshly composed from memory and clouds.
Now you can say the shape of your desire.

Now you believe that each sidereal item
carries a left-hand banner to describe
through curl and dissipation how it was,
that every friend is summoned by a name,
even in parting. You are wrong, and right
about the frail parabolas of love.

WEST WIND II

Snow too deep to shovel, wind so hard
it tears the empty bird's nest from its brief
refuge behind the gutter. You're immured
in books, and I'm half-witted by the life
of scholarship, half-silenced by the word.
The baby weeps and cheers and races off
to sleep at midnight, leaving us so tired
only our dreams declare us man and wife.

You know the tawny, hot, insistent voices
that thrilled the countryside near Módena
were not the true cause of our sleeplessness
that night. So now, in winter's sure decline,
warm in your arms, pressed hard against your flesh
and bone, I hear those nightingales begin.

EDEN

In lurid cartoon colors, the big baby
dinosaur steps backwards under the shadow
of an approaching tyrannosaurus rex.
"His mommy going to fix it," you remark,
serenely anxious, hoping for the best.

After the big explosion, after the lights
go down inside the house and up the street,
we rush outdoors to find a squirrel stopped
in straws of half-gnawed cable. I explain,
trying to fit the facts, "The squirrel is dead."

No, you explain it otherwise to me.
"He's sleeping. And his mommy going to come."
Later, when the squirrel has been removed,
"His mommy fix him," you insist, insisting
on the right to know what you believe.

The world is truly full of fabulous
great and curious small inhabitants,
and you're the freshly minted, unashamed
Adam in this garden. You preside,
appreciate, and judge our proper names.

Like God, I brought you here.
Like God, I seem to be omnipotent,
mostly helpful, sometimes angry as hell.
I fix whatever minor faults arise
with bandaids, batteries, masking tape, and pills.

But I am powerless, as you must know,
to chase the serpent sliding in the grass,
or the tall angel with the flaming sword
who scares you when he rises suddenly
behind the gates of sunset.

EMILY GROSHOLZ is the author of two collections of poems, *Shores and Headlands* and *The River Painter*. She has received grants from the Guggenheim and Ingram Merrill foundations, and is currently working on a fourth book of poetry. Associate professor of philosophy at Penn State and advisory editor at *The Hudson Review*, she lives in State College with her husband, Robert Edwards, and their son, Benjamin.

Designed by Martha Farlow

Composed by Brushwood Graphics, Inc., in Cochin

Printed by BookCrafters, Inc., on 60-lb. Booktext Natural